For Will, who slept—sometimes.   —CC

For Leigh, Donna and Florence,
who were with me from the beginning, middle and end.   —PT

PHILOMEL BOOKS
A division of Penguin Young Readers Group.   Published by The Penguin Group.
Penguin Group (USA) Inc., 375 Hudson Street, New York, NY 10014, U.S.A.
Penguin Group (Canada), 90 Eglinton Avenue East, Suite 700, Toronto, Ontario, Canada M4P 2Y3 (a division of Pearson Penguin Canada Inc.).
Penguin Books Ltd, 80 Strand, London WC2R 0RL, England.
Penguin Ireland, 25 St. Stephen's Green, Dublin 2, Ireland (a division of Penguin Books Ltd.).
Penguin Group (Australia), 250 Camberwell Road, Camberwell, Victoria 3124, Australia (a division of Pearson Australia Group Pty Ltd).
Penguin Books India Pvt Ltd, 11 Community Centre, Panchsheel Park, New Delhi - 110 017, India.
Penguin Group (NZ), Cnr Airborne and Rosedale Roads, Albany, Auckland 1310, New Zealand (a division of Pearson New Zealand Ltd).
Penguin Books (South Africa) (Pty) Ltd, 24 Sturdee Avenue, Rosebank, Johannesburg 2196, South Africa.
Penguin Books Ltd, Registered Offices: 80 Strand, London WC2R 0RL, England.

Text copyright © 2007 by Cynthia Cotten.   Illustration copyright © 2007 by Paul Tong.

Design by Semadar Megged.   The text is set in 24-point Stellar Epsilon.
The illustrations were rendered in oil on Arches watercolor paper.
Library of Congress Cataloging-in-Publication Data
Cotten, Cynthia.   Some babies sleep / Cynthia Cotten ; illustrated by Paul Tong.   p. cm.
Summary: Rhyming text reveals where different baby animals sleep, from a nest high in a treetop to a mother's snug pouch.
[1. Sleep—Fiction. 2. Animals—Infancy—Fiction. 3. Stories in rhyme.] I. Tong, Paul, ill. II. Title.
PZ8.3.C8284Som 2007   [E]—dc22   2006008919   ISBN 978-0-399-24030-0
10 9 8 7 6 5 4 3 2 1
First Impression

Some Babies Sleep

Cynthia Cotten

illustrated by **Paul Tong**

Philomel Books

Some babies sleep
high up in a tree.
Some babies rock
in the waves of the sea.

Some babies sleep
in a warm, cozy nest.

Some babies find
that a stall suits them best.

Some sleep in the desert,
some sleep in the snow,

some sleep in a meadow
where tall grasses grow.

Some babies sleep
in a pouch, safe and snug.

Some cuddle down
in a den that's been dug.

Some babies sleep
on the backs of their mothers.

Some curl up next to
their sisters and brothers.

Some sleep near a river,
some under the ground,

and some even sleep
in a cave, upside down.

Some sleep in the day,
some sleep in the night,

and some babies sleep
in a bed, tucked in tight.

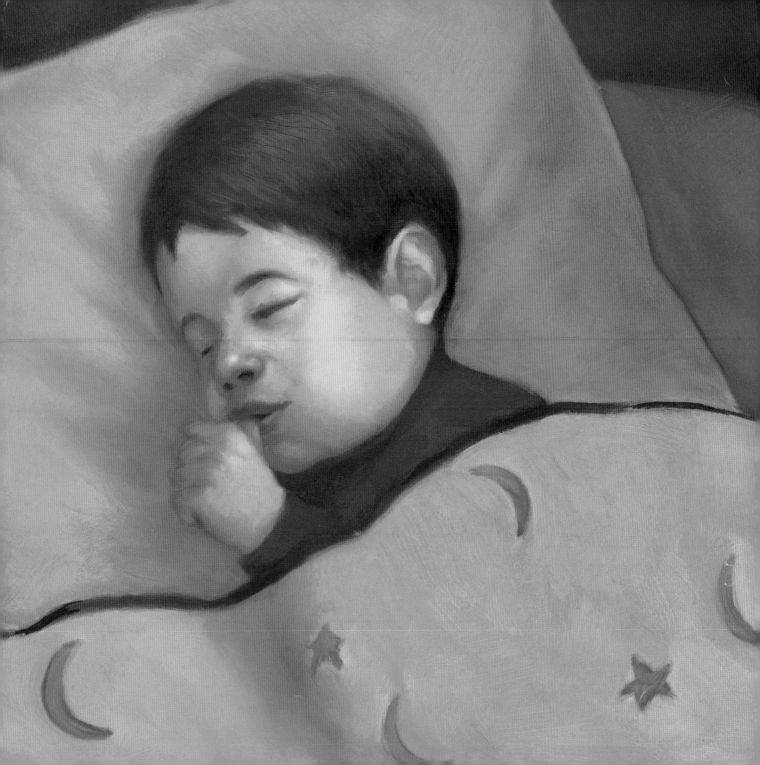

But whether they walk,
fly, swim, gallop, or creep,

All babies—
all babies—
all babies sleep.